Cupcakes & Romance

A Sweet & Clean Rewrite

Abiegail Rose

Abiegail Rose

Cupcakes & Romance

A sweet & clean rewrite of
"Love After Hours: Cupcakes & Kisses"

Shay runs Champagne Cupcakery, pouring her heart and soul into every cupcake. The sweet aroma of success is finally within reach as she lands a game-changing order—only to see her dreams crumble when the deal falls through, leaving her on the brink of losing everything.

Enter Stephen, her landlord and a man known for being tough in business. But behind his professional exterior lies a protective heart, especially when it comes to Shay. Drawn to her resilience and independence, Stephen sees more than just a tenant—he sees someone worth fighting for. Instead of demanding overdue rent, he offers her a lifeline: host a business networking event at her cupcakery, bringing new opportunities for both of them.

What begins as a simple business proposition soon stirs deeper emotions. Stephen can't help but be captivated by Shay's strength and the spark between them, but Shay is hesitant. Haunted by past hurts and an ex who refuses to let go, she's wary of opening her heart again—especially to someone as driven and dominant as Stephen.

In **Cupcakes & Romance**, a rewriting of the original novella *Love After Hours: Cupcakes & Kisses*, Shay and Stephen's journey intertwines faith, second chances, and the sweet possibility of love. As Shay battles her past and learns to trust again, she must decide whether to protect her heart or take a chance on a love as sweet and enduring as the cupcakes she bakes.

Shay and Stephen must discover if their love can be as sweet and enduring as the cupcakes that brought them together.

Prologue

Music from Alex Jean's latest album pulsed through the speakers, its uplifting beats filling the empty bakery. Amber and Miesha exchanged wide-eyed glances as they entered Champagne Cupcakery, instantly recognizing what the music meant.

Whenever Christian rap was playing, especially after hours, it could only mean one thing—Shalonda, or Shay as they called her, was deep into one of her new cupcake experiments. That usually meant they'd be taste-testing, something they always looked forward to.

As they made their way to the kitchen, they found Shay right in the middle of her creative zone. Standing at 5'6", with almond-brown skin that glowed in the kitchen light, Shay was piping frosting onto a fresh batch of cupcakes. Her long braids were tied back, swaying slightly as she moved to the rhythm of the music. She was so focused, she didn't even notice her friends standing in the doorway, smiling at the sight of her in action.

"Finally! I thought y'all were never gonna show up," Shay called out when she spotted them, her voice light with excitement. "I was about to eat all of these myself!"

Amber, tall and athletic with her short blonde curls, raised an eyebrow and smirked. "Looks like you already got a head start," she teased, pointing to the half-dozen cupcakes already surrounded by three champagne glasses.

Miesha, the smallest of the group but with a big personality, let out a deep, warm laugh. "No apron today, Shay?"

Shay looked down at her black v-neck shirt and flared jeans, both now dusted with flour and streaked with icing. "Oh no!" she groaned, laughing at herself. "I was so focused on trying out this new recipe, I completely forgot."

Amber shook her head and chuckled. "You know, this is why your dry cleaner probably prays over you every week."

The three women laughed together, the sound filling the space with warmth and joy. For a moment, Shay paused to take it all in. These moments, filled with laughter, friendship, and creativity, were blessings she never took for granted. Thank You, Lord, for these friends and this life, she prayed silently, feeling a deep sense of gratitude.

"Alright, ladies, let's get to it," Shay said, motioning them over to the counter where her latest creation was waiting. The cupcakes, topped with a delicate swirl of frosting, shimmered under the kitchen lights.

The three friends gathered around the kitchen island, each picking up a brightly wrapped cupcake, ready to continue their tradition. As they prepared to toast, Shay lifted her cupcake with a grateful smile.

"To faith and friends," she said, her voice steady and full of meaning.

Amber raised hers next. "To love and patience," she added with a wink.

Miesha grinned as she joined in, her voice full of determination. "To freedom and finances!"

Their cupcakes clinked together in unison, a sweet echo of their shared bond. Then, with a shared nod, they each took a bite, savoring the sweet, rich flavors that Shay had worked so hard to perfect.

As the smooth frosting melted on her tongue, Shay closed her eyes, letting the moment settle deep into her heart. She thought of the challenges she faced every day as a business owner, the constant pressure to succeed. But in moments like these—surrounded by friends who stood by her, supported her, and celebrated her wins—she knew God was with her, guiding her every step.

She whispered a prayer of thanks, not just for the success of her bakery but for the friendships that filled her life with joy. Lord, thank You for these moments, for the strength to pursue my dreams, and for the people You've placed in my life to walk this journey with me.

Whatever the future held, Shay knew one thing for sure: God would carry her through.

Unforeseen Circumstances

The day had been productive, and Shay thought she'd finally turned a financial corner. Yet, as she sat in her office at the end of the day, her eyes remained fixed on the computer screen, her heart sinking lower with each passing second.

Champagne Cupcakery Business Checking

Shalonda Brown, Owner

-$5,676.68 Current Balance

The numbers blurred in front of her eyes, flashing in harsh red that made her stomach twist. Just yesterday, her account had shown over ten thousand dollars. How could everything have changed so quickly?

Lord, I don't understand what's happening, she prayed silently, her hands resting on the edge of the desk, trembling. *Please show me a way out of this mess.*

Shay's mind raced. She'd been so careful with her finances, making sure every dollar was accounted for. Her heart pounded as she stared at the negative balance, her mind refusing to accept it.

Without hesitating, she picked up the phone and dialed the customer service number for Greenville's First National Bank, tapping her nails against the desk as the hold music played in her ear. She couldn't afford to wait long, but she knew she had no choice but to stay patient.

Philippians 4:6, she reminded herself, whispering the scripture under her breath. *Do not be anxious about anything, but in every situation, by prayer and petition, with thanksgiving, present your requests to God.*

After what felt like an eternity, a cheerful voice broke through the static.

"Hello, this is Cindy. Thank you for calling Greenville's First National Bank. How may I assist you today?"

"My name is Shalonda Brown," Shay said, trying to keep the rising panic out of her voice. "I'm the owner of Champagne Cupcakery, account number 243-123-4567. I'm showing a negative balance of over $5,000, and it was positive yesterday. What happened?"

There was a pause as Cindy typed on her end, and Shay held her breath, her grip tightening on the phone. She didn't want her employees, who were just outside closing up the shop, to hear the stress in her voice. This wasn't their problem; it was hers.

"Hmm, let me take a look at that for you," Cindy replied. "I'll be right back."

More hold music. Shay stood up and paced the small office, trying to keep her emotions in check. *God, I need Your peace right now. Please help me through this.* She felt a lump rise in her throat, but she swallowed it back, unwilling to let herself cry just yet.

After a few long minutes, Cindy's voice returned, less chipper this time. "Thank you for holding, Ms. Brown. It looks like your account was garnished today to cover an unpaid loan."

Shay's heart dropped. *The loan.*

Her mind raced back to the memory of Bryan, her ex, convincing her to cosign a loan for his remodeling business almost two years ago. She hadn't thought about that in a long time. She didn't want to. But now, it was coming back to haunt her in the worst way.

"I didn't take out a loan," Shay said quietly, her voice barely above a whisper. "At least, not for myself."

She could almost hear Cindy nodding on the other end. "Right, it shows that you cosigned a loan, and the borrower hasn't made a payment in over six months. The bank garnished your account to cover the overdue balance."

Shay closed her eyes and inhaled deeply, fighting back the frustration building inside her. *Lord, give me strength.* Bryan had always been unreliable, but she hadn't expected his bad choices to follow her this far.

"How much more is owed?" Shay asked, her voice steady, though her heart was pounding.

"Well, the good news is that your account has been brought current," Cindy replied. "There's no remaining balance on the loan."

Shay let out a slow breath, grateful that at least this part of the ordeal was over. "Thank you," she said simply, ending the call.

She leaned back in her chair and stared at the ceiling, closing her eyes. *Lord, I know You've carried me through worse than this, but right now, I'm really struggling to see how to move forward. Please show me a way.*

Just as she was gathering her thoughts, a soft knock at the door startled her. Before she could answer, the door creaked open, and Amber's familiar voice cut through the silence.

"Girl, what is going on? You look like you've seen a ghost."

Shay turned to see her best friend standing in the doorway, her arms crossed over her chest and a concerned expression on her face. Amber's green eyes scanned the room, and it didn't take long for her to zero in on the laptop screen behind Shay, where the negative balance still flashed in red.

"Come on, sit down," Shay waved her over, trying to force a small smile.

Amber walked over and sat across from her, her blonde curls bouncing as she leaned forward. "Alright, spill it. What's going on?"

Shay sighed, her voice barely above a whisper. "Bryan."

Amber's eyes widened in surprise. "Bryan? What does he have to do with this?"

Shay ran her hand through her braids and shook her head, still trying to wrap her mind around the situation. "Remember that loan I cosigned for him? The one I shouldn't have?"

Amber's mouth dropped open. "You mean the one I specifically told you not to cosign?"

"Yeah," Shay muttered, her face falling. "He defaulted on it. The bank garnished over fifteen grand from the bakery's account to pay it off. Now I'm over five thousand in the red."

Amber blinked, silent for a moment, before letting out a deep breath. "Well, that's one way to start the evening."

Shay groaned, leaning her head back. "I know."

Amber reached over and gently placed a hand on Shay's. "Look, this isn't the end of the world. I know it feels like it, but God's not gonna let you go down because of Bryan's mistakes. We've got the Smith wedding this weekend, and that's ten grand. We'll be back in the black by Monday."

Shay bit her lip, grateful for Amber's optimism. "Yeah, you're right. I just... I can't believe I let this happen."

Amber squeezed her hand. "It's not your fault, Shay. And it's not too big for God to handle. You've got a good business, and this is just a setback, not a dead end."

Shay nodded, her heart lightening just a little. Amber was right. She had faced challenges before, and God had always seen her through. This was no different.

"Thanks," Shay whispered. "I really needed to hear that."

Amber smiled, pulling her friend into a quick hug. "Of course. Now let's get out of here and clear our heads. How about ice cream and a movie? Netflix has that new Christian film we've been talking about."

Shay chuckled softly. "I couldn't agree more."

As they left the office and headed toward the door, Shay sent up one last prayer: *Lord, I trust You to work all things for good. Help me walk through this with grace, and give me peace, even when I don't understand the path ahead.*

Meeting Mr. Taylor

The past week had been a blur of busy days and restless nights. Champagne Cupcakery's sales had been strong—especially after the successful launch of Shay's latest cupcake flavors. But despite that, Shay still found herself struggling to catch up on rent. Salaries had been covered, but rent was another story entirely.

God, please help me through this. I don't know what I'm going to do, she prayed silently as she pulled up in front of the towering office building where her landlord, Stephen Taylor, worked.

Shay had never been late with rent before. Not once in the fifteen months she had leased her space. But now, with everything that had happened—Bryan's loan, the garnishment of her bank account, and the sudden loss of a wedding contract just days ago—she was short. Five grand short. She had no choice but to face the music and hope for some grace.

Shay stepped out of her car and looked up at the building, the Taylor Investment Properties logo emblazoned across the gleaming glass. The twelve-story structure loomed over her like a silent judge, and Shay squared her shoulders, forcing herself to take a deep breath. She had a plan, after all. She had dressed to impress in her pink pantsuit, paired with a black Champagne Cupcakery tee and black pumps, determined to look as professional as possible.

Lord, give me the words, she prayed again, silently, as she stepped through the large glass doors of the building.

Inside, everything was sleek and modern—white walls, polished chrome accents, and floors so clean they reflected the light from the oversized windows. Shay approached the front desk, where a friendly-looking older woman greeted her with a smile.

"Good morning, welcome to Taylor Investment Properties," the receptionist said warmly. "How may I assist you?"

Shay forced a smile. "Hi, I'm here to see Mr. Taylor. I'm one of his tenants—Shalonda Brown from Champagne Cupcakery."

"Of course," the receptionist replied, nodding as she picked up the phone. She dialed a few numbers and glanced up at Shay. "I'll just let his assistant know you're here. One moment, please."

Shay nodded politely and waited, her heart pounding as she tried to steady her nerves. She silently whispered a prayer, asking for peace in this meeting. She didn't want to appear desperate, even though she was barely holding it together on the inside.

"Ms. Brown?" the receptionist said, interrupting her thoughts. "Mr. Taylor is ready to see you now. Just take the elevator up to the twelfth floor, and his assistant will meet you at the reception area."

"Thank you," Shay replied, accepting the key card the receptionist handed her. She made her way to the elevator, her heels clicking softly against the marble floor. Once inside, she followed the instructions, pressing the button for the twelfth floor and inserting the key card.

As the elevator ascended, Shay closed her eyes for a brief moment. *Lord, I trust You,* she reminded herself. *You've gotten me this far, and I know You won't leave me now.*

When the doors opened, she stepped into a reception area that was just as sleek and modern as the rest of the building. A tall, redheaded woman—Gina, Mr. Taylor's assistant—greeted her with a professional smile.

"Ms. Brown? Please follow me," Gina said, leading her down a long hallway. "Normally, Mr. Taylor doesn't handle these matters personally, but he's seeing tenants this week. You picked the right time to come by."

Shay nodded, feeling both relieved and nervous. As they reached the last door at the end of the hall, Gina knocked lightly before opening it.

"Mr. Taylor, Ms. Brown is here to see you."

Shay stepped inside, and for a moment, she froze. Standing behind the desk was Stephen Taylor himself, tall and imposing, with a commanding presence that immediately made her heart race. He was handsome, no doubt—his almond-brown skin gleamed under the office lights, and his brown eyes held an intensity that was hard to look away from.

He smiled politely as he stepped around the desk to greet her, extending his hand. "Miss Brown, it's nice to meet you. I'm Stephen Taylor. What can I do for you today?"

Shay took his hand, feeling a slight jolt at the contact. She cleared her throat, trying to gather her thoughts. "Yes, thank you for meeting with me, Mr. Taylor. I'm the owner of Champagne Cupcakery, one of your tenants on Main Street."

He nodded, gesturing for her to sit down. "Please, have a seat."

Shay sat down, her palms slightly sweaty as she smoothed her pants and took a breath. God, give me strength.

"So, Miss Brown," Stephen said, taking his seat across from her. "What brings you here today?"

Finally finding her voice at the zing that rushed through her body, Shay spoke, "Yes, yes, I'm so sorry." She shook her head clearing the fog in her mind caused by his hands and face. "Yes. So I came to see you today. I've been, I've been a tenant of yours for almost a year and a half. And for the first time ever, we are experiencing some financial issues which means that I won't be able to make rent this upcoming month. So, I wanted to come to you directly and figure out the best way to remedy this."

Stephen sat down across from Shalonda at his desk and looked at her. His fingers interlaced under his chin before replying, "Normally, your lease says that if monies are not paid within five days of the due date, then the eviction process is started. We are very strict on that policy here at TIP."

She took a deep breath and hung her head, not knowing what she was going to do. She loved her business. It was the first thing that she was truly good at. She did not want to give up or fail. *Everything had been going perfect, and then Bryan had to go and ruin everything as he always did.*

As she fought back tears of defeat, Stephen studied her and took in her presence.

"So, Miss Brown, you're a baker. Is that right? Tell me more about your business and what it is that you do."

Shay's head snapped up. "Oh, yes, of course," she said, "I would be happy to. So obviously we're Champagne Cupcakery. We are open for lunch, dinner, and intimate gatherings. We serve gourmet cupcakes paired with champagne or wine. So, each beverage that we serve complements a certain type of cupcake. We do new pairings each day."

"Hmm," he said, "That's definitely unique, not something I've ever heard of before. How did you come up with this idea?"

"Well, actually it's funny. My best friend Amber loves champagne, and I love cupcakes. So whenever I would bake, she would bring over a new bottle of champagne. After a lot of experimenting, we got to know which champagnes or wines really worked well with which types of cupcakes I would make. I always had a love for baking, and it just grew from there."

"Wow, that's quite the story." Stephen leaned back in his chair and really looked at Shalonda. "You know what, Miss

Brown, I think I may have an idea on how we can help your business and how you can help me in the process. Why don't I go with you back to your bakery, and you can show me around? Show me what you've done with the place since the remodel. I haven't been in there since it was just four walls."

Shalonda jumped up, ready to hug him across the desk, but she held herself in check, "Oh my God, of course, yes, yes, yes! I would love to do that. Obviously, you already know our address. I will meet you there. Do you want to do this today?"

He looked at his watch. "Yes, today will be perfect since I'm done for the day. I'll meet you there."

A Knight in a Suit

Thirty minutes later, Shay stood in the front of her bakery, wiping her hands nervously on her apron. She had just finished the lunch rush, and now, her heart raced as she waited for Stephen to arrive. She glanced at the clock on the wall and inhaled deeply.

Lord, give me peace. I don't know how this will go, but I trust You, she prayed silently, calming herself with each breath.

A moment later, the chime of the doorbell announced Stephen's arrival. Shay's heart skipped a beat as she watched him step into the bakery, looking effortlessly polished in a tailored navy suit. His presence commanded attention, and she couldn't help but notice how heads turned as he entered.

Focus, Shay, she reminded herself, pushing aside her nerves.

"Welcome to Champagne Cupcakery," she greeted, walking up to him with a smile. "I'm so glad you could make it."

Stephen smiled back, his dark brown eyes scanning the bakery's bright, welcoming interior. "Thanks for having me, Shay. I've been looking forward to seeing what you've done with the place."

The way he said her name made her pulse quicken, but she pushed the feeling aside and focused on her role as the professional business owner she was. "Come on in, I'll give you the tour," she said, motioning for him to follow her.

"Thank you so much for doing this. Come in, come in. Let me definitely show you around. As you know, the bakery is 5000 square feet. And of that, 3500 square feet of it is seating. We have intimate seating on one side for couples who come at night for dessert. Then we have seating on the other side, for those who come in groups or with families. We have two counters. A fast serve counter on the right-hand side for those who know what they want. On the other side we have the display case for those who want custom orders, catering, or who don't quite know what they want, so they would want more assistance from one of the cupcakers."

Stephen nodded, impressed. "You've created a really welcoming space here, Shalonda. It's got a great vibe."

"Thank you, but please call me Shay." She smiled and blushed under his compliment and stare. "Thank you. That's exactly what I wanted—for people to feel like they can come in, relax, and enjoy themselves."

"And the cupcakes?" Stephen asked, his curiosity piqued.

Shay's face lit up as she led him to the display case. "We bake everything fresh daily. Whatever doesn't sell, we donate to the local shelter. I've always believed in giving back to the community, and it's a small way we can help."

"That's a great way to avoid waste and do something meaningful," Stephen said, admiration in his voice. "So, what's your best seller?"

Shay didn't hesitate. "Triple milk chocolate. It's rich, decadent, and—"

"Probably too sweet for me," Stephen interrupted, smiling.

Shay raised an eyebrow playfully. "Oh? Not a fan of sweet?"

"I like sweet, but I prefer a little spice," he admitted. "Even in desserts."

Shay grinned. "In that case, you'll have to try our spicy dark chocolate cupcakes. They're rich, but with a kick. I'll make sure you get a batch next time."

"I'll hold you to that," Stephen said, his eyes locking with hers for a moment. There was something unspoken between them—a shared spark of interest. But before Shay could dwell on it, Stephen shifted the conversation back to business.

"I have to say, this place is impressive," Stephen remarked, walking around the bakery with his hands in his pockets. "It'd be a shame to see you struggle over one tough month."

Shay swallowed hard, trying not to let the weight of her financial stress overwhelm her. *God, thank You for bringing me this far,* she reminded herself. *I trust You to carry me the rest of the way.*

"Thank you," she said softly. "I've poured everything I have into this bakery. I can't imagine doing anything else."

"It would be a shame to see you close down due to a financial setback when it seems you're doing so well," Stephen said, walking around. He thumped his index finger gently on his chin. Before he stopped to turn and look at her. "I have an idea."

"Okay! What is it? I am game for almost anything." She spoke eagerly, bouncing on the balls of her feet.

"Well, hear me out first," he chuckled. "So, what I'm thinking is this... Why don't we start a business after hours networking group? We'll use your bakery as the location. This will help you bring in funds. It will also help me get leads for my commercial property units."

Shay slowly nodded her head as she thought it over, "Yes. Yes! That would be amazing. Of course, this sounds like something that could work. When did you want to get started on it, Mr. Taylor?"

He smiled. "I would like to get started on it within a couple weeks. So why don't you do some brainstorming and then we will connect within the next week."

"All right. That sounds like a plan, Stephen. I am so happy that you're working with me and that you're giving me this opportunity. I promise I'll do my best and I won't let you down."

Stephen smiled, his expression softening. "I have no doubt that you will."

As they finalized their plans, Stephen gave her one last lingering look before he left. "We'll meet next Friday to go over the details. I'll have my assistant send over some promotional materials so you can start spreading the word."

Shay nodded, still processing how quickly everything had come together. "Thank you again, Stephen. You don't know how much this means tome."

Stephen gave her a knowing look. "You deserve this chance,Shay. I'm looking forward to seeing what you can do."

After he left, Shay stood in the middle of the bakery, feeling a sense of overwhelming gratitude. She whispered another prayer, her heart full. *Lord, thank You for opening this door. I'm trusting You with everything—my business, my future. Please continue to guide me through this.*

Admitting the Truth

The lunch rush was in full swing, and the line at Champagne Cupcakery stretched all the way to the door. Shay could hardly keep up with the orders as customers eagerly bought her latest creation—Funfetti gourmet cupcakes paired with sparkling rosé. Business was booming, but even with the buzz, Shay couldn't shake the thoughts running through her mind. Her upcoming partnership with Stephen Taylor loomed large in her head.

Lord, help me focus on the blessings before me, she prayed as she hurriedly packaged another order.

Just as the rush began to slow, the chime of the doorbell signaled Miesha's arrival. Shay looked up, immediately feeling lighter as her friend walked in, beaming with energy as usual.

"Hey, girl!" Shay called, grabbing a Green Matcha Tea cupcake and a glass of Sauvignon Blanc, Miesha's usual order, and setting it aside for her.

Miesha made her way to her favorite spot in the back of the bakery, her sleek bob bouncing as she moved. Shay followed her after finishing up with the last customer, eager for a break.

The moment Shay joined her, Miesha wrapped her in a bearhug, squeezing tightly enough to make Shay grunt. "You know I needed this break," Miesha said, releasing her and diving straight into her cupcake. "I don't know what you did today, but girl, do it again! You had so many people in your line that it even boosted candle sales at my shop."

"That's awesome," Shay said, smiling. "Things are looking up. I just hope it continues."

Miesha glanced at her friend, noticing the hint of worry in her voice. "You okay, Shay? I know you've had a lot on your plate."

Shay sighed and sank into her chair, her gaze drifting toward the counter where Stephen had stood just a few days earlier. She hadn't been able to stop thinking about him—or the way her heart seemed to race whenever he was around.

Focus on what matters, she reminded herself. But the truth was, Stephen had gotten under her skin.

"I'm fine," she finally replied, though her voice betrayed her uncertainty. "I've just been thinking about... stuff."

Miesha raised an eyebrow. "Uh-huh. What kind of 'stuff'? Is this about that fine Mr. Taylor?"

Shay's cheeks flushed, and she avoided Miesha's gaze. "It's not like that."

"Girl, please," Miesha said with a laugh, taking another bite of her cupcake. "You can't fool me. I see how you light up when you talk about him. You can't deny that something's going on."

Shay sighed, running a hand through her braids. "I don't know, Miesha. I mean, yes, he's been really helpful, and I appreciate everything he's done, but... I don't know if I'm ready for anything more than business right now. Not after everything with Bryan."

Miesha's expression softened, and she reached across the table to take Shay's hand. "I get it, Shay. You've been hurt, and you're trying to protect your heart. But don't let the mistakes of your past hold you back from something that could be a blessing."

Shay looked down at their joined hands, feeling a lump rise in her throat. Miesha was right. She had been guarding her heart so closely that she hadn't allowed herself to consider the possibility of something new—something better.

Lord, give me the wisdom to know what to do, she prayed silently, her heart aching with the weight of her uncertainty.

"Maybe you're right," Shay admitted quietly. "But it's just...complicated. I don't want to mess things up. Stephen and I have a business relationship, and I don't want to jeopardize that."

Miesha smiled gently. "If God's got a plan for you and Stephen, He'll guide you through it. Trust Him. You don't have to figure it all out today."

Shay nodded, feeling a little more at peace. Miesha had away of reminding her to keep her focus on God's will, even when her emotions felt tangled.

"I'll pray about it," Shay said. "Thanks, Mie."

"Always, girl," Miesha replied, giving her hand a reassuring squeeze. "Now, let's plan a girls' night this weekend. Amber and I want all the details!"

Shay laughed, grateful for her friends' support. "You got it."

Later that evening, as Shay sat in the quiet of her living room, her mind wandered back to her conversation with Miesha. The truth was, she couldn't deny the growing attraction she felt toward Stephen. But with the memories of Bryan's betrayal still fresh, she wasn't sure she was ready to open her heart again.

Lord, help me see clearly, she prayed, leaning back on her couch. *I don't want to let fear hold me back, but I also don't want to make a mistake. Give me the strength to trust You in this.*

Her phone buzzed on the coffee table, and she picked it up to see a text from Amber.

Amber: So... what's the deal with Mr. Taylor? Miesha told me you've been acting all shy and weird about him. Spill the tea!

Shay chuckled and shook her head, typing out a quick reply.

Shay: Not much to tell. He's helping me with a networking event for the bakery. Strictly business, I promise!

Amber: Yeah, right. I know you better than that.

Shay smiled and sighed. She knew her friends meant well, but the thought of exploring her feelings for Stephen felt overwhelming. She needed time—time to pray, time to reflect, and most of all, time to trust that God's plan would reveal itself in His timing.

Lord, I'm placing this in Your hands, she whispered, setting her phone down. *If Stephen is meant to be part of my life in a deeper way, show me how to move forward. And if not, give me peace with that, too.*

With that prayer on her heart, Shay stood up and headed to bed, feeling a sense of calm settle over her. Whatever the future held, she knew she wasn't walking this path alone. God was with her every step of the way.

A Personal Dilemma

The only thing that had been on Stephen's mind since meeting Shay was her—her energy, her passion, and her determination. He leaned back into his executive chair, remembering how her copper eyes had lit up when they talked about the networking event.

Stephen smiled, recalling how Shay's enthusiasm had filled the room. Her confidence was refreshing. She wasn't just another tenant—she was someone who truly believed in what she was building. That alone intrigued him.

It wasn't just her appearance that stayed with him, though. There was something deeper about her. The fire and drive she had for her work spoke volumes about who she was—a woman of strength, ambition, and focus. Shay, as she preferred to be called, had a magnetic presence that drew him in. It wasn't just the way she looked in that hot pink suit, though she wore it with style and grace. No, it was more than that. It was her spirit. She had a confidence that intrigued him, made him want to know more about the woman behind the bakery.

But he caught himself before his thoughts went too far. *Lord, help me keep my focus on what matters. This is business first,* he reminded himself. Stephen had always been intentional about honoring God in his relationships, and he wasn't about to let his emotions get in the way of his professionalism.

The sound of his assistant's voice through the P.A. system interrupted his thoughts.

"Mr. Taylor... Mr. Taylor!" Gina called.

Stephen blinked, snapping out of his reverie. "Oh, yes. Sorry about that, Gina. What can I do for you?"

"Joe is here to see you... about your plans for marketing."

"Okay, send him in."

Moments later, Joe strolled into the office with his usual casual energy, pouring himself a cup of coffee before sitting down. "Hey, man, what's good?" he greeted Stephen, leaning back comfortably in the chair across from him.

Stephen chuckled. "What's good? Just planning some things for the upcoming event. I've got a tenant, Shay

Brown, who owns Champagne Cupcakery. We worked out a deal—she's behind on rent, so we're hosting a business networking event at her bakery. It's a win-win: she gets new clients, I get the rent, and we might even find some potential clients for your residential real estate deals."

Joe raised an eyebrow. "Sounds solid. But man, you've got this far-off look like there's more to this story. Who is this Shay?"

Stephen smiled but hesitated for a moment. "She's.. . impressive. Hardworking, focused, and really driven to succeed. She's built something special with her bakery."

Joe leaned forward, watching him closely. "Uh-huh. And?"

Stephen let out a breath, trying to articulate what he was feeling without crossing any lines. "Look, it's not just about her business. She's... she's someone I admire. She's got this fire, this passion for what she does. It's hard not to be drawn to that."

Joe grinned knowingly. "So, what are you going to do about it?"

"She's focused on her business, and I'm focused on mine," Stephen said firmly. "It's about making sure we both succeed."

"Hmm," Joe muttered, watching Stephen carefully. "But you like her, don't you? I mean, you're talking about her like she's something special."

Stephen hesitated again, his thoughts swirling. Was there something deeper about his interest in Shay? Sure, she was beautiful, and her drive was attractive, but he couldn't let his feelings get in the way of what was ultimately a professional relationship. His faith had taught him the importance of honoring people in the right way, keeping things above board.

He sighed, finally meeting Joe's gaze. "She's impressive, no doubt. Smart, driven, and yeah, she's... she's beautiful. But more than that, I see potential in what she's building, and I want to support that."

Joe raised an eyebrow, a knowing smile playing on his lips. "So, what are you going to do about it?"

Stephen sat back in his chair, thoughtful. "For now? I'm going to stick to business. I've got to be wise about this. She's a tenant, and I want to see her succeed. I'll keep my feelings in check and trust that God will lead me where I need to go—whether that's in business, or otherwise."

Joe chuckled, raising his glass. "Sounds like you've got your head on straight. But man, if you do like her, don't let fear hold you back. Just remember—God's got a way of surprising us when we least expect it."

Stephen nodded, appreciating Joe's advice. But for now, he was content to leave things in God's hands. If there was more to his connection with Shay, he would trust God to reveal that in time. Until then, he had work to do.

Stephen chuckled softly. "I'm going to stay focused. It's business for now. But... I was thinking about asking her to dinner—to finalize the details for the event."

Joe raised his eyebrows, his grin widening. "Dinner, huh? That's a good way to mix business with... whatever else you've got brewing."

Stephen shot him a look. "It's about the event, Joe. Nothing more."

Joe held up his hands, clearly amused. "Sure, man. Keep telling yourself that."

Stephen couldn't help but smile at his friend's teasing. But deep down, he knew this dinner was more than just business. There was something about Shay that stirred something in him—a sense of admiration, maybe even something more—but he wasn't about to rush anything. *God, if there's more here, You'll guide me through it*, he prayed silently.

"Look, I just want to be respectful and see where things go," Stephen said finally, his tone more serious. "If there's anything more, I'll trust God to make it clear."

Joe nodded, giving him a pat on the back. "That's the right mindset, man. If it's meant to be, it'll work out. But hey, good luck with dinner. Keep it professional, but don't be afraid to let her know you see her as more than just a business partner."

Stephen smiled and nodded. "Thanks, Joe. We'll see how it goes."

Later That Day

Shay wiped down the last of the counters, her mind still buzzing with ideas for the upcoming networking event. She was excited but also nervous about how it would all come together. Just as she was locking up for the night, her phone buzzed. It was a text from Stephen.

Hey Shay, hope you're doing well. I was thinking we should finalize the details for the networking event. How about dinner Friday night? We can discuss everything then. Let me know if you're available!

Shay's heart skipped a beat. Dinner? She wasn't sure what to make of it. Was this just business, or was there something more behind the offer? She thought back to their conversations. Stephen had always been professional, but there had been moments—little looks, small gestures—that hinted at something deeper.

Lord, give me wisdom here, Shay prayed quietly. *I don't want to read too much into this, but if there's something more, show me how to handle it with grace.*

After a moment, she texted back.

That sounds great! I'm free then. Just let me know the time and place.

Almost immediately, his reply came.

Perfect. I'll make a reservation for 7. I'll text you the details. Looking forward to it.

Shay smiled, setting her phone down. Dinner with Stephen. She didn't know where this would lead, but she trusted God to guide her through it—whether it was strictly business or the beginning of something more.

With a soft sigh, she closed the bakery, whispering a prayer as she left. *Lord, I trust You. Whatever comes next, I know You'll be with me.*

Internal Battles

"What am I going to do about this?" Shay whispered to herself as she lay in bed, staring up at the ceiling. Her mind just wouldn't let go of thoughts about Stephen—Mr. Taylor, as she kept reminding herself to call him.

But then there was the way he insisted she call him Stephen. His broad shoulders, his calm confidence, and the way his presence filled the room. She couldn't deny that her heart skipped a beat when he had lightly touched her back, sending a warmth down her spine she hadn't expected.

Lord, help me keep my focus, she thought, feeling frustrated with herself. *He's giving me an opportunity to fix this mess that*

Bryan caused. I can't let my emotions get in the way of what's really important here.

All week, Shay had struggled to sleep, tossing and turning through endless thoughts. She had prayed about it each night, asking God for clarity, but her mind kept circling back to Stephen. It wasn't just his appearance—although he was undeniably handsome—but there was something about his integrity and the way he respected her as a businesswoman that made her heart stir.

By the time Friday rolled around—the day she was supposed to meet Stephen for dinner to finalize the plans for the networking event—Shay felt completely unprepared. Her thoughts had been consumed all week, and now she was feeling the pressure to present herself confidently, both as a professional and... well, she didn't want to think too much beyond that.

As the day flew by, she found herself staring at the clock, realizing she had less than an hour before she had to meet him. And despite all the time she'd had to prepare, she still couldn't decide what to wear. Each backup outfit she considered felt either too casual or too formal, and she didn't want to send the wrong message.

Frustrated, Shay poked her head out of her office door. "Amber... Amber!" she called through the empty bakery. "I need your help, now!"

"I'm coming!" Amber called back from the front of the-bakery, where she was closing up for the day. She walked into Shay's officewith the day's receipts in one hand and a pencil behind her ear, lookingamused. "What's up?"

Shay let out a sigh. "I have that dinner with Mr. Taylor tonight, and I don't know what to wear."

Amber raised an eyebrow, smirking slightly. "And why, exactly, do you need to change?"

"What do you mean, why?" Shay asked, staring at her friend with confusion.

"Why do you need to change out of your work clothes just for dinner?"

Shay opened her mouth to respond but hesitated. "I mean... Iwant to look nice," she finally said.

"Uh-huh," Amber said, crossing her arms with a knowing look."Let me guess—you've got a little crush, don't you?"

Shay's eyes widened in protest. "What? No! Come on, Amber, it's not like that. It's just dinner to go over plans for the event."

Amber grinned. "Sure, okay. But you've been talking about this guy non-stop for days now. And you never change out of your work clothes for anyone—certainly not when you were with Bryan. So why now?"

Shay frowned, trying to come up with a good reason, but Amber's point made her pause. "Look, Stephen's a profession-al. I just don't want to look out of place. He's probably taking me somewhere nice, and I need to make a good impression. That's all."

Amber lifted her chin and gave her a teasing smile. "Right. No crush at all. Got it."

"Amber!" Shay groaned. "It's just business. He's giving me a chance to fix things at the bakery. End of story."

Amber shook her head, laughing softly. "Uh-huh. Whatever yousay. But just in case, wear the long black maxi dress. It's perfect. It can be casual or dressy, depending on where you're going. You'll look great and feel comfortable."

Shay sighed in relief. "Thank you. I really needed your help."

Amber started to leave, but not without one last grin. "Love you, girl. But seriously, just be yourself tonight. You've got this."

"I love you, too," Shay called after her, grateful forAmber's support. But as she turned back to the mirror, she couldn't help butwonder if Amber was right. Was this just business—or was there something more stirring between her and Stephen?

Lord, give me clarity tonight, she prayed quietly. *Help me see this for what it is and give me the wisdom to keep my heart in the right place.*

With that, Shay began to get ready, hoping the evening would bring answers.

Dinner

When Shay walked into Le Alexander's, Stephen's breath caught in his throat. She was beautiful. Her braids were styled in a neat bun on top of her head, and the long black maxi dress she wore flowed gracefully as she moved. There was an elegance about her that went beyond her appearance, and it struck him as she approached.

"Hello again," she greeted him warmly, offering her hand. "It's so good to see you. I hope I dressed okay for tonight."

Stephen smiled, clearing his throat. "You look amazing, Shay. More than okay." He quickly caught himself, hoping he hadn't said too much. "Why don't we head to our table?"

"That sounds like a plan," she agreed.

Stephen gently guided her forward with a light touch on the small of her back, feeling a surprising warmth shoot through him. He pulled his hand away, slightly taken aback by the sensation. Lord, help me keep my focus on the purpose of tonight, he prayed silently, scratching his palm as they made their way to the hostess.

As they followed the hostess to their table, Stephen berated himself. Keep it together, man. This is about business, not feelings. Focus on the event and the opportunity to help her get back on track. Let everything else fall into place later, if it's meant to be.

When they arrived at the table, Stephen pulled out Shay's chair for her, then moved to his side of the table, unbuttoning his suit jacket as he sat down. "So, how's business been?" he asked, ready to get the conversation started.

Shay's face lit up, and she couldn't hold back her excitement. "Business has been amazing! We launched a new funfetti cupcake paired with a rosé, and the line was out the door and down the block. We're catching up financially, and with this networking event, I'm expecting to be not just in the black, but well into profitability."

"That's fantastic to hear," Stephen said, genuinely impressed. "You've really turned things around. After we order, we can dive into the event details. But for now, why don't you tell me a little more about yourself? I know about Champagne Cupcakery, but I'd like to know about you. Are you from Greenville originally?"

Shay laughed lightly. "Yeah, I'm a Greenville girl through and through. I went to high school here, and that's where I met Amber, my best friend and bakery manager. She encouraged me to start the bakery, and now she handles the day-to-day operations so I can focus on creating new cupcake combinations. It's been a blessing. And even though I've traveled for vacations, I never wanted to live anywhere else."

Stephen nodded, smiling. "I get that. Greenville has its charm. I haven't lived here all my life, though. I moved here from New York when I was 21 and bought my first property. Now, at 33, I've built a real estate portfolio around the area."

Shay raised her eyebrows, clearly impressed. "Wow, that's incredible. You've built quite an empire."

Stephen chuckled, humbled by her words. "I've had my share of failures along the way. Real estate just happened to be the one thing I was good at."

Shay looked at him thoughtfully. "I can't really picture you failing at anything."

He laughed. "Trust me, I've failed plenty. It's part of the journey."

Their conversation flowed easily, and soon the waiter arrived to take their orders. Shay ordered first, her voice confident. "I'll have the lobster pasta with a glass of Chardonnay. No salad, but could we have extra bread, please?"

Stephen smiled, surprised and amused by her choice. "I'll have the same," he said, before the waiter left.

Once the waiter was gone, Stephen couldn't resist asking, "So, extra bread, huh?"

Shay grinned. "Oh, absolutely. I love bread. Plus, with how much I work out, I need the carbs to keep my energy up. I'm all about maintaining and building strength."

Stephen raised an eyebrow, even more intrigued. "I'm the same way. I do a lot of weightlifting, boxing, and Krav Maga to stay in shape."

Shay's eyes lit up. "That's amazing! I've been doing boxing and weight training too. It's my favorite way to stay active."

Stephen smiled, feeling a deeper connection with her. He found himself drawn to her passion for life, her energy, and her grounded nature. But he quickly refocused his thoughts. This is about the event. Stay on track, he reminded himself, clearing his throat.

"Okay, let's get into the event details," he said, shifting the conversation. "What ideas do you have for the networking event?"

Shay drummed her cupcake-painted nails lightly on the table as she spoke. "So, I was thinking we charge $20 for each networking ticket. Each ticket will include a cupcake and a glass of wine or champagne, depending on the pairing for the night. We'll keep it simple—one lighter cupcake with champagne or white wine, and one richer cupcake paired with red wine. That way, everyone can choose based on their preferences."

She paused, looking at Stephen for feedback. He nodded for her to continue.

"With the space in the bakery, we can fit about 100 people. At full capacity, we'd make $13 profit per ticket, which comes out to about $1,300 a night. If we host the event every Friday for four weeks, we'd make $5,200 in a month. That's more than enough to cover rent!"

Stephen listened closely, impressed with her attention to detail. "I love that idea. You've thought this through really well."

She smiled, relieved. "I figured we could greet guests as they arrive, then hand things over to one of our assistants for the announcements. I was also thinking we could do a raffle, and the winner would get a dozen cupcakes and a bottle of champagne as a thank-you."

"Great idea," Stephen said, nodding in approval. "And we can promote the event a few ways: selling tickets on your website, putting up signs in your bakery, advertising in the local paper, and using social media to spread the word."

"Perfect!" Shay agreed, her enthusiasm returning. "It sounds like we have a solid plan."

Stephen smiled. "We definitely do."

As the conversation shifted back to lighter topics, Shay suddenly remembered something. "Oh, I almost forgot—I baked something for you! I didn't bring it here because I wasn't sure how they'd feel about me bringing food into the restaurant, but I have it for you afterward."

Stephen's eyebrows lifted. "You baked me something?"

Shay nodded, smiling. "You mentioned you liked chocolate and spicy foods, so I made you some spicy dark chocolate cupcakes. And I paired them with a bottle of Merlot to thank you for believing in me and giving me this opportunity."

Stephen's heart warmed at her thoughtful gesture. "You're something else," he said, genuinely touched.

Just as their conversation was about to continue, the waiter arrived with their meals. But before Shay could dig in, Stephen gently laid his hand on the table, palm up.

"Hold on," he said, smiling at her. "Let's pray."

Shay blinked, caught off guard but grateful. She placed her hand in his, bowing her head as Stephen began to pray.

"Dear Lord, we thank You for this food and the opportunity to share this meal together. Bless it to our bodies, and thank You for good company, good friendship, and the opportunities You've provided for us. In Jesus' name, amen."

"Amen," Shay echoed, feeling the warmth of his hand lingering in hers as they looked at each other for a brief moment.

Dessert

"Thanks for coming back to the bakery with me," Shay said as she led Stephen through the back door and into the kitchen. The familiar smell of fresh cupcakes filled the air. "I left the cupcakes to cool, so all I have to do is ice them, and they'll be ready for you."

Stephen followed her, taking in the warmth of the space. He admired how much care she put into everything, from her baking to her business. It wasn't just a job for her—it was her passion.

Shay walked over to the fridge, pulled out a piping bag full of chocolate icing, and motioned for him to join her at the counter, where the spicy dark chocolate cupcakes were neatly arranged. "Now you get to see how the magic happens," she said with a laugh.

"I'm ready," Stephen said, smiling at her enthusiasm.

Shay pushed the icing toward the tip of the bag with her hands, carefully piping it onto the cupcakes with a steady precision that came from years of practice. When she finished, she looked at him with a proud smile. "Ta-da!" she exclaimed playfully.

But as she pulled the piping bag away, she accidentally brushed it against her cheek, leaving a smear of chocolate across her skin. Stephen noticed and, without thinking, gently reached out and wiped the chocolate off her cheek with his thumb.

Shay froze for a moment, her heart racing at the unexpected touch. She hadn't realized how much Stephen's presence had affected her until that moment. His kindness, his strength, and the way he treated her with such respect stirred something deep inside.

Stephen, too, felt the electricity between them, but he kept his gaze soft and respectful. He wiped the chocolate from his thumb, savoring the taste, but his attention was fully on Shay. Their eyes met, and there was a silent understanding—something unspoken but undeniably real.

Without thinking, Stephen took a small step closer, his hand still hovering near her face. He moved slowly, giving Shay every chance to pull away if she wanted to. But she didn't. Instead, she found herself leaning in slightly, her heart pounding with a mix of anticipation and uncertainty.

Stephen gently placed the icing bag on the counter and stepped even closer. He reached out, carefully wrapping one arm around her waist, his movements slow and deliberate. Shay could feel her pulse quicken, but there was no fear—only a quiet sense of trust.

"Shay..." Stephen whispered, his voice full of emotion. He paused, searching her face to make sure this was what she wanted.

She met his gaze, her voice barely a whisper. "Stephen, I—"

But before she could finish, Stephen gave her lips the gentlest kiss as gently pulled her closer, their foreheads almost touching. "I care about you," he said softly leaning back, his hand resting lightly on her back. "But I don't want to rush this. I don't want you to ever feel like this is about anything more than getting to know you... for who you are."

Shay's heart fluttered at his words. She hadn't expected this level of honesty and respect, and it only made her care for him more. "I appreciate that, Stephen," she said, her voice sincere. "I've been through a lot, and I don't want to rush into anything either. But... I do feel something here. I just don't know what to do with it yet."

Stephen nodded, understanding her hesitation. "That's okay," he said quietly. "We don't have to figure it all out tonight. Let's take our time. We'll let God guide us through this."

Shay felt a sense of peace wash over her at his words. She knew he meant it—that he wasn't just saying what he thought she wanted to hear. There was a depth to his faith, and it mirrored her own.

"Thank you," she whispered, grateful for the way he was handling things. "I don't know what this is yet, but I'm open to seeing where it leads."

Stephen smiled, relieved that they were on the same page. He gently pulled away, giving her space to breathe. "Let's just keep things simple. We'll focus on the business for now, and whatever happens beyond that... we'll trust God to show us the way."

Shay smiled softly, appreciating his thoughtful approach. "That sounds like a good plan."

They stood there for a moment, the tension easing into something comfortable and reassuring. Stephen looked over at the cupcakes she had made, then back at her.

"You know," he said, breaking the silence with a playful grin, "I'm really looking forward to these cupcakes. Spicy chocolate? You weren't kidding when you said you remembered my favorite flavors."

Shay laughed, the moment of seriousness giving way to lightheartedness again. "I'm glad you like them. It was the least I could do to thank you for all your help."

Stephen's eyes softened. "You don't owe me anything, Shay. I'm just glad we're working together. Whatever happens next, I'm here."

Just then, the oven timer dinged in the background, and Shay snapped back to reality. "Oh, looks like my next batch is ready!" she exclaimed, hurrying toward the oven.

Stephen chuckled as he watched her move with ease and grace. There was something so genuine about her, something that drew him in. But tonight wasn't about rushing things. It was about building trust, friendship, and, maybe down the road, something more.

As Shay pulled the cupcakes from the oven, Stephen couldn't help but whisper a quick prayer. *Lord, guide us through this. Help us walk this path with wisdom and patience.*

Shay turned back to him with a smile. "Well, I hope you're ready to taste these. I'm pretty sure they're going to knock your socks off."

Stephen laughed, grateful for the lighthearted end to the evening. "I'm ready. Let's see if these cupcakes live up to the hype."

As they enjoyed the moment, Stephen knew one thing for certain: whatever this was, it was in God's hands. And he was willing to wait and see where it led.

Wanting More

"Come in," Joe shouted when they heard a knock at the door of Stephen's office.

Stephen turned from the whiteboard, where he had been sketching out ideas for the upcoming event, just in time to see Gina enter with a box in hand.

"What's this?" Stephen asked, his curiosity piqued.

Gina, always eager for a bit of gossip, smiled knowingly. "Appears to be a special delivery from Miss Brown." She placed the box of cupcakes, a bottle of wine, and a small card on Stephen's desk, casting a hopeful glance for any insight into the mysterious delivery.

"Thanks, Gina," Stephen replied, keeping his voice neutral. "That'll be all."

Once the door closed behind her, Joe turned toward Stephen with a mischievous grin. "So... how did last night go?"

Stephen sighed, crossing the room to examine the cupcakes Shay had sent. He traced his hand over the box thoughtfully before answering, "Not quite how I expected."

Joe raised an eyebrow. "Oh? Do tell."

Stephen chuckled softly, more at himself than the situation. "I told myself I was going to keep things professional, take it slow. But as the night went on, I realized I couldn't deny my feelings anymore. I tried to express that, but Shay wasn't ready for it."

"Wait a minute," Joe interrupted, holding up his hand. "So, let me get this straight: You've got a woman who's grateful, beautiful, and from what you've said, clearly enjoys your company. You took her out to dinner, and she sends you home with cupcakes. But when you tell her you're interested, she doesn't want anything serious?"

Stephen nodded. "Yeah, that's about it. She was honest about where she's at. She's been through a lot, and she told me she needs more time. She's not sure what she's ready for, and I can respect that."

Joe leaned back in his chair, clearly puzzled. "And how do you feel about that? I mean, it sounds like she's into you, so why not just... you know, see where it goes?"

Stephen shook his head. "That's not how I work, Joe. I don't want something casual. If I'm going to be with someone, I want it to be meaningful. I don't want her to think this is just about attraction or convenience. She's worth more than that."

Joe gave him a long look, then nodded. "I respect that. You've always been the kind of guy who wants more than surface-level stuff. But still, man, it's got to be tough."

Stephen let out a slow breath, leaning against the desk. "It is tough. But honestly, I'm grateful she was upfront. She's been through a lot, and I don't want to pressure her into something she's not ready for. I just... I don't want to rush things. I'm trusting that God will guide us both."

Joe studied his friend for a moment, then chuckled softly. "You're a rare breed, man. Most guys would see this as the perfect setup. But you—nah, you want the real deal. You've got your head on straight."

Stephen smiled. "Thanks, Joe. I've just learned that if something's going to last, it has to be built on more than just feelings or timing. I want Shay to know that if this is going to be something real, I'm willing to wait. I want her to feel secure in that."

Joe shook his head with a grin. "Man, if anyone can show her what a real relationship looks like, it's you. But what's the plan now? Just wait and see?"

"Exactly," Stephen replied, his voice steady. "I'm going to give her the time and space she needs. I'm not going to push her into anything. But I also believe there's something special here, and I'm willing to be patient and let God guide us through it."

Joe raised his coffee cup in a mock toast. "To patience and faith, my friend."

Stephen laughed, lifting the box of cupcakes in response. "And to Shay's spicy chocolate cupcakes."

Second Thoughts

Champagne Cupcakery had been bustling all day. Every time Amber tried to ask Shay about her dinner with Stephen, another customer or employee interrupted, making it impossible for Shay to respond. It wasn't until they were finally closing up that the opportunity arose.

Shay was wiping down the counters in the back when Amber snuck up behind her and tapped her on the shoulder. "So, are you finally gonna tell me how it went?" Amber asked, grinning.

Shay glanced at her friend with a small smile, then turned back to the counter. "Oh... well, it was fine," she replied, continuing to clean.

Amber raised an eyebrow. "Uh-huh. Fine? That's all I get? How about the dress—did he like it?"

Shay nodded. "Yeah, he liked the dress."

Amber crossed her arms, clearly not buying it. "Okay, what's going on? You, Miss Chatty, are giving me two-word answers. Something's up. Spill it."

Shay sighed, knowing her friend wouldn't let it go. Amber was relentless when it came to anything involving relationships. "Fine. We went back to the bakery after dinner, I made him some cupcakes... and we kissed."

Amber's eyes went wide, and she let out a gasp. "Oh my gosh! You guys kissed? Right here?"

Shay nodded again, biting her lip.

Amber's jaw dropped. "No way! My girl is finally letting herself loosen up a little."

Shay chuckled softly, but shook her head. "Nothing else happened. We stopped after that."

Amber tilted her head. "Okay, why? I'm guessing it was you who pulled back?"

"You would be wrong," Shay admitted, putting the towel down and turning to face her friend. "He told me he wanted me, Amber."

"Well, that's kind of romantic," Amber teased with a wink.

"No, not just physically," Shay explained, her expression growing more serious. "He told me he respected me and that he wanted me—as in, a real relationship. He wasn't playing games. He was completely honest."

Amber's smile softened, sensing the weight of Shay's words. "And what's the problem with that?"

"The problem," Shay began, her voice quiet, "is that I'm not ready for that. I don't think I want that right now."

Amber blinked, clearly surprised. "Wait... You're telling me you have a guy who's not only one of Greenville's most eligible bachelors, but he's also interested in something real—something serious—and you told him no?"

Shay shrugged, feeling a bit uncertain but standing by her decision. "I did. I told him I'm not ready for anything serious right now. I've been through a lot, and I just... I need more time."

Amber stared at her for a long moment, clearly trying to process it. "Girl, you've got a man who's successful, good-looking, and clearly upfront about his feelings for you. Most women would jump at the chance. Are you sure you're making the right choice?"

Shay nodded firmly. "I know it sounds crazy, but I need to be sure I'm ready to move forward before I commit to anything.

I can't start something with him unless my heart is fully in it—and right now, I'm just not there."

Amber softened, recognizing the sincerity in Shay's voice. "Okay, I get that. You've been through a lot, and you're trying to protect yourself. But you should at least think about it, Shay. A guy like that doesn't come around every day."

Shay smiled, appreciating her friend's concern. "I know. And I have thought about it. But for now, I think I just need to be friends with him. I want to take things slow, and when the time is right—if it's right—I'll know."

Amber shook her head, half in disbelief but half in admiration. "Well, you're stronger than most people, I'll give you that. I just hope you're not closing the door on something good."

"I'm not closing the door," Shay assured her, leaning back against the counter. "I'm just being careful. I need to be in the right place before I can even think about being in a relationship. Stephen deserves that honesty, and so do I."

Amber smiled, her teasing nature fading into genuine support. "I get it. And I respect that, Shay. Just promise me you won't let fear keep you from something great when the time comes."

Shay nodded. "I promise."

Amber grinned. "All right, then. We'll see how this plays out."

With that, the two friends finished cleaning up the bakery, but Shay's mind lingered on the conversation. She had made the right choice—for now. But in her heart, she knew she'd have to face those feelings again, and when the time was right, she'd trust God to lead her where she needed to go.

Trying It Out

"Okay, enough of the moping around!" Amber declared a few days later, tired of watching Shay look distracted and downcast. "Why don't you just call him and tell him you changed your mind? You're clearly still thinking about it."

Shay sighed, pausing from her task of wiping down the counters. "I don't know, Amber. I wouldn't even know what to say. And the more time that passes, the more foolish I feel about it all."

Amber raised an eyebrow. "The Shalonda I know wouldn't give up on something she wants."

Shay let out a small snort. "Yeah, and that's how I got into this situation to begin with. I don't want to make things worse."

As if on cue, the distinct smell of something burning wafted through the kitchen. "Oh no!" Shay cried out, rushing to the oven.

Amber gasped. "Shay! That's the third batch of cupcakes you've burned today!"

Shay groaned, pulling out the tray of charred cupcakes. "I'm so off my game today."

Amber clucked her tongue in sympathy. "Why don't you take a break from baking and help with the front? You need to clear your head, girl."

Shay nodded, feeling the weight of her distracted thoughts. She had never burned cupcakes before, and here she was, ruining batch after batch. "Yeah, maybe you're right."

She transitioned to the front of the bakery, hoping the change in scenery would help. But even while ringing up customers, her thoughts kept drifting back to Stephen. Since their dinner, she hadn't been able to get him out of her mind, especially the way he had respected her boundaries. To top it off, the cupcakes she had dubbed "his cupcakes"—the spicy dark chocolate ones—were selling like crazy.

As she was ringing up another order, Shay wondered if Stephen had received the delivery she had sent to him. Did he like the cupcakes? Did he want more than just cupcakes?

And then, as if her thoughts had conjured him, there he was—Stephen, standing at the counter, looking effortlessly put together in his khakis, white button-up, and blue pullover. He smiled warmly at her, and for a moment, she froze.

"Hey, Shay," Stephen greeted her, his tone casual but his eyes focused on her. "I was wondering if you had any more of those spicy cupcakes." He winked, and Shay felt her nerves ease.

"For you, of course," she replied, offering him a shy smile. She quickly retrieved two cupcakes from the display case, placing them on plates. As she handed them over, she let Amber know she'd be taking a break to talk with Stephen.

They sat down at one of the tables near the back, where the shop was quieter. Stephen leaned forward, his expression softening. "I got the cupcakes and the Merlot," he said. "Both were amazing, but... I couldn't stop thinking about the person who made them."

Shay felt her heart skip a beat as his words sank in.

"I've been thinking about you, too," she admitted, her voice soft.

Stephen smiled, his eyes lighting up. "Can you take off for a bit? I was hoping we could spend some time together. Maybe go over some ads?"

Shay glanced around the bakery, noticing the steady flow of customers. She was about to decline, but before she could say anything, Amber appeared at her side, untying her apron strings with a knowing smile. "Go," Amber insisted. "I've got this."

Shay grinned at her friend, handing over the apron. "Okay, okay, you don't have to convince me!"

Stephen mouthed a silent thank you to Amber as Shay joined him.

Later That Day

Shay and Stephen had spent the last few hours at his place, surprisingly focused on the business at hand—going over ad copy for the networking event. Shay chuckled to herself, amused that their time together had turned into reviewing flyers, but she couldn't deny how comfortable she felt with him.

"I like the one on the right," she said, pointing to a mock-up Stephen was holding.

"Me too," Stephen agreed. "Looks like we're on the same page."

"So, what else do we need to cover?" Shay asked, leaning back on the couch.

Stephen sat beside her, setting the flyers down. "We just need to finalize a date for the first event. How does Friday after next sound? Is that enough time for you to prepare?"

Shay thought for a moment. "Yeah, I think that works. Amber can update the website, and you can handle the marketing."

"Perfect," Stephen said, smiling. "I'll have Gina get the ads out first thing Monday."

Shay nodded, feeling a sense of accomplishment now that the event was coming together. But before she could say anything, Stephen jumped up. "How about dinner? I can order something in—Chinese, Italian, hibachi..."

Shay laughed. "I'm not really hungry."

Stephen paused, peeking around the kitchen corner with a playful look of disappointment. "No? Then... are you ready to leave?"

Shay shook her head, standing up and walking over to him. "No, I'm not ready to leave either."

Stephen's expression softened as she approached. Shay placed her hands on his arms, sliding them up to rest around his neck. "I don't want to leave... I want to be here with you," she whispered.

Stephen's breath hitched, but he remained steady. Gently, he placed his hands around her waist, pulling her closer. "Shay..." he murmured, his voice filled with emotion.

Shay closed her eyes as he leaned in, their foreheads touching. But this time, Stephen didn't rush. He kissed her slowly, tenderly, letting her know through his touch that he was in this for the long haul.

They stayed like that for a long moment, simply holding each other. It wasn't about passion or urgency—it was about trust and connection.

When they finally pulled apart, Stephen smiled at her. "I meant what I said. I'm willing to take this slow. I don't want to rush you into anything. We'll figure this out, together."

Shay felt her heart swell with gratitude. "I appreciate that, Stephen. I don't know what the future holds, but I'm willing to try this out—with you."

Stephen's face lit up, and he pulled her into a tight embrace. "That's all I needed to hear."

Networking

Shay and Amber buzzed around the bakery, making last-minute adjustments to the decor for the debut networking event. The excitement in the air was palpable, and everything was coming together.

"Girl, I can't believe how quickly time has flown," Amber exclaimed, fluffing the last of the bows on the cupcake table.

"Who are you telling?" Shay replied with a grin. "It feels like just yesterday Stephen and I were planning this, and now we're an hour away from kicking it off."

"Right? And every single ticket for the next three events is sold out. We made rent and then some!"

Shay laughed. "Yeah, I'd say things are looking up."

Amber smirked and added with a teasing tone, "Plus, you're showing up to work all happy and singing these days. I'm guessing things with Stephen are going well too?"

Shay threw a decorative bow at her friend. "Amber, seriously! Don't start."

"I'm just saying, girl! The past two weeks have been good to you. It's like you're walking on clouds. You haven't burnt a thing since you started dating him!" Amber teased, playfully.

Shay shook her head, laughing. "It's been amazing, I'll give you that."

Amber gave her a knowing look. "Yeah, I can tell. But don't let it get to your head. You know love makes you act a little crazy sometimes."

Shay raised an eyebrow. "Who said anything about love?"

"Oh, come on," Amber sang, dancing around the room with a grin. "I've known you since we were teenagers. You can't tell me you don't loooove him."

Shay laughed, rolling her eyes. "Okay, let's not get carried away. How about we stick with 'really like'? The big 'L' word is too soon."

Amber just smiled. "Call it whatever you want, but from where I'm standing, it sure looks like he loves you. And I'm not saying you're in love, but... you care about him. You're happy."

Shay shrugged, smiling softly. "We're just two adults who really like each other. Let's not make a big deal of it."

"I'm not making a big deal of it, Shay! I'm just saying, I'm happy for you. You deserve this. All of it—things are turning around for the bakery, and your personal life is flourishing too."

Shay chuckled. "I appreciate that. But let's focus on the event, shall we?"

"Fine, fine," Amber relented with a laugh. "But seriously, you owe me a raise after this. And maybe an introduction to some of that premium man meat like Stephen."

Shay laughed, shaking her head at Amber's antics. "Actually, Stephen's business partner, Joe, is coming tonight—and yes, he's single. I'll put in a good word."

Amber's eyes lit up. "Oh, I'll be ready! Just point me in his direction."

As Amber hurried off to freshen up, Shay took a moment to admire the bakery. The two cupcake stations were perfectly set up, the prize table was ready with business card bowls, and the decorations—navy blue and white—looked elegant and professional. Everything was ready.

Well, almost everything. She glanced down at her clothes and realized she still needed to change before Stephen arrived.

Later That Evening

Stephen arrived right on time, his eyes immediately finding Shay in the crowd. As soon as he saw her, his face broke into a wide smile. "Wow, you look amazing," he said, admiring her pinstriped dress and matching jacket.

Shay blushed, doing a little twirl for him. "Thanks! How did you know I'd be wearing pinstripes?"

Stephen chuckled. "I didn't, but I'm not complaining. Do you mind if we match?"

"Not at all," Shay replied, smiling. "Maybe it'll let everyone know I'm taken."

Stephen winked. "Oh, so you're claiming me now?"

"Claiming? Please, Mr. Taylor. You've been claimed," she teased, leaning in to kiss him briefly on the cheek.

"Later," she whispered, pulling back just enough to keep things respectful but letting him know the chemistry between them was still very much alive.

Stephen grinned. "Later," he agreed, his eyes twinkling with mischief.

"All right, let's get to work. People are already showing up, and I thought we'd greet everyone for the first half-hour before turning it over to Gina."

"Sounds perfect," Stephen said, taking her hand as they made their way toward the front entrance.

Misunderstandings

The networking event was in full swing. The bakery was buzzing with people from all around town—business owners, entrepreneurs, and professionals exchanging cards, making connections, and enjoying the cupcakes and wine pairings.

Stephen's hand rested gently on the small of Shay's back as they moved through the crowd, stopping to introduce each other and shake hands with guests. Everything was going smoothly until a deep voice called her name.

"Shay!"

She froze, the familiar voice sending a jolt of surprise through her. Turning around, she found herself face-to-face with Bryan—her ex. Her face scrunched in confusion. "Bryan? What are you doing here?"

He stepped closer, completely ignoring Stephen's presence. "Hey babe, I missed you," Bryan said, pulling her into an unexpected hug.

Shay stiffened, uncomfortable with the sudden physical contact. Stephen was quick to react, gently pulling Shay back into his protective embrace. He extended his hand to Bryan, his tone calm but firm. "Hi, I'm Stephen. Who are you again?"

Bryan gave Stephen a once-over, then took his hand for a brief shake. "Bryan. Shay and I go way back," he said, flashing a smug smile.

Shay rolled her eyes. "Yeah, way back... in the past. Bryan, this is Stephen—my boyfriend."

Bryan's eyes widened in surprise. "Boyfriend, huh? So, you've moved on..."

Shay crossed her arms. "Yes, I have. And if you don't mind, this isn't exactly the place to have this conversation."

Bryan shrugged, unfazed. "I just thought, you know, after you paid off my loan, that you were finally coming to your senses. Figured it was your way of showing you wanted me back."

Shay's mouth dropped in disbelief. "You really are full of yourself, aren't you?" she muttered, shaking her head. "Good-bye, Bryan." She grabbed Stephen's hand, pulling him toward the kitchen, mumbling under her breath, "Unbelievable... the nerve of that guy..."

Once they were out of earshot, Stephen turned to her, his expression unreadable. "So... is Bryan the reason you didn't want to be with me? The reason you couldn't pay rent?"

Shay sighed, knowing this moment was inevitable. "Yes, he is. He made some bad decisions, and I trusted him. But it's over. I've moved on."

Stephen nodded slowly, his face still hard. "I see."

"What do you mean by that?" Shay asked, frowning.

Stephen exhaled sharply. "Nothing. Let's just finish this night and then I'll get out of your way. How about you work one side of the room and I'll take the other?"

"Stephen, wait, let's talk—" she started, but before she could finish, Stephen turned and walked back into the crowd, leaving her standing alone in the kitchen doorway, confused and a little scared that he had gotten the wrong idea.

Shay spent the rest of the night trying to focus on the event, but her eyes kept drifting toward Stephen. He was distant, keeping to his side of the room, avoiding her. Her heart sank as she replayed the encounter with Bryan over and over in her mind, wondering where things had gone wrong.

"Shay, this event is amazing!" Amber gushed, coming over to her friend with excitement. "Oh, and by the way, Stephen's business partner Joe? He's hot! Why didn't you tell me?"

Shay forced a smile, but her mind was elsewhere. "Amber, we have a problem. Bryan is here."

Amber's eyes widened. "What? Why didn't you tell me? I could've kicked him out!"

Shay shook her head. "He's a paying customer, Amber."

"So? He still owes you money!"

"I know, but... I just hate confrontation. Let's just let it be."

Amber's expression softened. "Shay, I get it. But you know he's the reason Stephen's been avoiding you, right?"

Shay's heart sank further. "I think so. Bryan said some stupid things, and Stephen overheard... Now I think he's questioning everything."

Amber groaned. "That guy is a total idiot. You want me to fix this?"

Shay hesitated. "I don't know how to fix this, Amber."

Amber grabbed her arm with determination. "Come on, I'll help you sort this out. Let's go talk to Stephen."

Together, they left the bakery, hoping to clear up the misunderstanding before it caused any more damage.

Winning His Heart

Shay stood in front of the mirror, adjusting the soft fabric of the sundress she had chosen. It wasn't fancy, but it was one of her favorites—a simple, floral pattern that made her feel both comfortable and confident. Tonight wasn't about looking perfect; it was about being real with Stephen. She took a deep breath, hoping that the gesture she had prepared would show him just how much he meant to her.

On the dresser, she glanced at the small framed photo she had placed there—a picture of the two of them from a spontaneous day at the local carnival. It had been such a simple moment, filled with laughter and lightness. They had taken the photo at a carnival photo booth, and it had become one of her favorite memories. The picture captured Stephen mid-laugh, his arm around her, and Shay's wide, genuine smile.

This wasn't about grand gestures; it was about reminding him that, despite the ups and downs, they shared something real. And she was ready to show him that she was willing to try—willing to take the next step.

Amber's advice still echoed in her mind.

• Cut outfit? Check.

• A thoughtful surprise? Check.

• Ready to speak from the heart? Almost there.

Shay picked up her phone and typed out a message:

> Hey, I really need your help with something. Can you come over? I promise it won't take long.

Her heart raced as she waited for his reply. After the tension from the networking event earlier in the night—particularly Bryan's unexpected appearance—she knew they needed to clear the air. She didn't want to let the situation fester, but she also didn't want to rush into anything without explaining how she really felt.

Chirp.

Stephen's text came through:

You sure you don't already have enough help? You and Bryan seemed pretty close at the event.

Shay winced. Of course, Bryan's presence had left Stephen feeling uneasy, and she couldn't blame him. But she needed to make sure he understood where things stood between her and Bryan. She quickly replied:

I don't know what Bryan was thinking, but he's in the past. I left with Amber right after everything. Please, Stephen, I really need your help. Can you come over?

After a few long minutes, Stephen finally responded:

OMW, be there in 20.

Shay exhaled, feeling both nervous and hopeful. Now it was time to show Stephen she was ready to be serious, in her own way.

Twenty minutes later, there was a knock at the door. Shay's heart leaped as she hurried to open it. Standing there was Stephen, his face a mixture of curiosity and hesitation. Clearly, the events of the night were still weighing on him.

"Hey," he greeted her, stepping inside.

"Hey," Shay replied softly, closing the door behind him. "Thank you for coming."

Stephen gave her a brief nod but didn't say much. "What's going on, Shay? You said you needed help?"

Shay motioned for him to sit on the couch, her hands fidgeting slightly. "I do. But not with the bakery or anything like that." She sat down next to him, trying to keep her voice steady. "I need to clear the air about what happened at the event."

Stephen's eyes softened a little, but there was still a guardedness in his posture. "I'm listening."

Shay reached over to the side table and picked up the framed photo she had prepared. She held it in her lap, looking down at the picture before handing it to Stephen. "Do you remember this?"

Stephen's brow furrowed as he took the frame from her. His expression softened as he looked at the photo. "This was from the carnival," he said, his voice quieter now. "That was a fun day."

Shay smiled, recalling the memory. "It was. We were so carefree that day. No worries, just laughter and... being ourselves."

Stephen nodded, his gaze still on the photo. "Yeah, I remember."

Shay took a deep breath, gathering her thoughts. "That's why I wanted to give you this," she said, pointing to the picture. "I know things have been a little heavy lately, especially tonight. And I haven't done a great job of being clear about how I feel. But I wanted you to know that... I'm ready to try. I want to build something real with you, Stephen. Slowly, carefully—but real."

Stephen's expression softened further as he looked from the picture to Shay. "You've been holding back," he said, though not accusingly. "I could feel it. But I didn't know why."

Shay nodded, her hands trembling slightly. "I have been. I've been scared, Stephen. Scared of getting hurt again, scared of letting someone in. But I don't want to keep letting that fear stop me. I care about you, and I'm ready to take this seriously. I want to build something—like the way we were in that picture. Happy, carefree, but with something deeper."

Stephen placed the photo down on the coffee table and turned to her, his hand reaching out to gently take hers. "Shay, I told you before—I'm willing to take things slow. I want to build something real with you, not rush into anything. I respect your boundaries."

Shay's heart swelled with gratitude. She had been so nervous, but now, with Stephen sitting beside her, she felt a sense of peace. "Thank you," she said, her voice barely a whisper.

Stephen smiled, his tension easing as well. "Of course. We'll figure this out together, one step at a time."

Shay leaned her head on his shoulder, letting herself enjoy the warmth and comfort of his presence. "I'm sorry for the way I've handled things. I've been holding back because I've been afraid to get hurt again. But I don't want to keep letting that fear control me."

Stephen kissed the top of her head, his voice gentle. "We'll work through it, Shay. I'm not going anywhere."

For the first time in a long while, Shay felt hopeful about the future. She looked up at him, smiling. "I'm really glad you're here."

Stephen grinned, the playful sparkle returning to his eyes. "Well, since I'm here, how about we enjoy some of those famous cupcakes you're always talking about?"

Shay laughed, feeling the tension melt away. "I think that can be arranged."

As they stood to head into the kitchen, Stephen paused, pulling her into a gentle hug. "Shay, no matter what happens, just know that I'm here for you. I care about you, and I'm willing to take this journey at your pace."

Shay closed her eyes, hugging him back. "Thank you, Stephen. That's all I needed to hear."

Epilogue: A Year Later

Everyone gathered in front of the brand-new Champagne Cupcakery location, all smiles and excitement in the air. Shay stood proudly behind a bright red ribbon, holding an oversized pair of scissors as cameras clicked, capturing the big moment. Her heart swelled with gratitude—this was a dream come true.

To her left, Stephen stood with their friends, cheering her on with his usual supportive smile. Amber bounced up and down with enthusiasm, unable to contain her excitement.

"Yay!" Amber cried out, clapping her hands and grinning from ear to ear.

Stephen chuckled at her energy, sharing a glance with Joe, who slipped an arm around Amber's waist, equally amused.

As the crowd gathered closer, Shay opened the oversized scissors and cut the ribbon, signaling the official grand opening of her second bakery. Applause erupted from everyone present, the joy of the moment palpable.

Once inside, as customers began to explore the new shop and taste the cupcake samples, Amber grabbed Shay by the hand and pulled her aside.

"Oh my goodness, Shay! You have no idea how proud I am of you," Amber said, her voice filled with emotion as she pulled her friend into a tight hug. "I love you so much, and I'm just... so proud of everything you've accomplished."

Shay hugged her back, grinning. "Well, you better hold on, because I've got something even bigger to tell you."

Amber stepped back, curiosity filling her eyes. "What? What could top this?"

Shay gripped Amber's hands, her smile widening. "You're running this new location too, Amber. And starting today, your salary gets a 30% increase, plus you'll get 5% of each store's profits every month."

Amber's mouth fell open. "What?!"

Shay laughed. "You heard me! You've been by my side since the very beginning, and I can't think of anyone more deserving. With the new manager and the bakers coming on board, things are going to run smoothly here—and I trust you completely to oversee everything."

Amber stood in stunned silence for a moment before throwing her arms around Shay again. "Oh my gosh, Shay! I don't even know what to say. I'll make sure you never regret this. Thank you for believing in me."

Shay smiled, squeezing her friend's shoulder. "You've earned it, Amber."

Amber stepped back, wiping her eyes and trying not to cry as a watery grin lit up her face, "You're the best boss and friend anyone could hope for. But I need to take you to Stephen. He's waiting for you in the back."

"He's not in here?" Shay asked, surprised.

"Nope...," Amber said with a wink.

Curiosity piqued, Shay followed Amber toward the back of the bakery, passing through the crowd of happy customers and employees. As they walked, she exchanged greetings with her team, watching with pride as they served cupcakes and took orders.

When they finally reached the kitchen, Shay froze in her tracks.

The entire space was filled with roses—white, pink, and red—covering every surface. Shay's breath caught in her throat as she took in the sight. "Wow... How did you... when did you...?"

Stephen stepped forward, taking her hands in his, his eyes never leaving hers. "Do you know how much you've come to mean to me over this past year?" he asked softly.

Shay blushed at the intensity of his gaze, nodding silently, too overwhelmed to speak.

Stephen smiled gently, his voice filled with warmth and emotion. "When you have something—or someone—important in your life, you cherish them. You protect them. You make sure they know just how much they mean to you."

Before Shay could respond, Stephen slowly got down on one knee. Tears filled her eyes as she realized what was happening.

"Oh my God..." she whispered, her hand covering her mouth.

Stephen took a deep breath, his eyes never leaving hers. "Shalonda Melissa Brown, I think I fell for you the first day you walked into my office. You've challenged me, inspired me, and brought so much joy into my life. You're everything I never knew I needed—my missing piece. I love you, Shay, and I want to spend the rest of my life with you. Will you marry me?"

Tears spilled from Shay's eyes as she smiled down at him. "Yes! Yes! Yes!" she exclaimed, her voice shaking with emotion.

Stephen slipped the princess-cut diamond ring onto her finger, and Shay immediately dropped to her knees, wrapping her arms around him. She held his face in her hands and kissed him, pouring all her love and gratitude into that moment.

The crowd in the bakery cheered, clapping as they watched the proposal unfold. But for Shay and Stephen, it felt like they were the only two people in the world.

As they held each other, Shay whispered, "This is the perfect ending to an incredible day. I love you so much."

Stephen grinned, his arms tightening around her. "This is just the beginning, Shay. The best is yet to come."

And with that, their future, filled with faith, love, and new beginnings, seemed as sweet as the cupcakes that had brought them together.

The End

Hello, Dear Readers!

I truly hope you've enjoyed diving into this sweet & clean rewrite **Cupcakes & Romance**. It's been such a joy to bring Shay and Stephen's story to life, and I'm grateful to have shared it with you. If their journey of love, second chances, and sweet moments has left you smiling, I also hope it's stirred up another craving—one for cupcakes, kisses, and perhaps a glass of champagne or wine to pair with them!

As you know from Shay's Champagne Cupcakery, there's nothing quite like the perfect pairing of a decadent cupcake with a refreshing sip of wine. Whether you're celebrating something special or simply indulging in a quiet evening of sweetness, the right combination can turn a simple treat into something magical.

To help satisfy your sweet tooth (and maybe inspire your own cupcake and wine pairing adventures), I've put together a list of my favorite pairings. These combinations bring out the best in both the cupcakes and the wines, making every bite—and every sip—an experience to savor.

Feel free to try these pairings at home, and don't hesitate to experiment with your own! After all, just like love, sometimes the best matches are the ones you never expect.

White Wines & Cupcake Pairings

Champagne and *vanilla bean cupcakes*: A classic pairing, the light and airy flavor of vanilla bean cupcakes is perfectly complemented by the effervescent bubbles of champagne.

Sparkling wine and *funfetti cupcakes*: For a playful and fun treat, nothing pairs better than the sweetness of funfetti with a lively sparkling wine.

Chardonnay and *strawberry cupcakes*: The creamy richness of Chardonnay beautifully enhances the fresh, fruity sweetness of a strawberry cupcake.

Sauvignon Blanc and *lemon cupcakes*: The crisp and citrusy notes of Sauvignon Blanc are a delightful match for the tangy brightness of lemon cupcakes.

Pinot Grigio and *salted caramel cupcakes*: The subtle sweetness of Pinot Grigio pairs wonderfully with the rich, buttery flavor of salted caramel.

Riesling and *vanilla or almond cupcakes*: With its natural sweetness, Riesling complements the delicate flavors of vanilla or almond cupcakes, creating a harmonious balance.

Pink champagne and *raspberry cupcakes*: A romantic pairing, the slight tartness of raspberry cupcakes is beautifully balanced by the blush and bubbles of pink champagne.

Red Wines & Cupcake Pairings

Port wine and *peanut butter cupcakes*: The bold, rich flavors of port are the perfect match for the nutty, creamy taste of peanut butter cupcakes.

Banyuls dessert wine and *cookies and cream cupcakes*: This sweet dessert wine pairs perfectly with the nostalgic flavors of cookies and cream.

Pinot Noir and *cinnamon cupcakes*: The earthy, light-bodied qualities of Pinot Noir elevate the warmth and spice of cinnamon cupcakes.

Shiraz and *red velvet cupcakes*: The bold, fruity profile of Shiraz complements the smooth, cocoa flavor of red velvet cupcakes.

Cabernet Sauvignon and *chocolate cupcakes*: The deep, robust flavors of Cabernet Sauvignon bring out the rich, bittersweet chocolate notes in a classic chocolate cupcake.

Merlot and *dark chocolate cupcakes*: A match made in heaven—Merlot's smooth, velvety texture perfectly complements the indulgent richness of dark chocolate.

Zinfandel and *carrot cake cupcakes*: Zinfandel's jammy, fruit-forward notes are an ideal pairing with the spiced sweetness of carrot cake cupcakes.

Non-Alcoholic Cupcake Pairings

Sparkling Apple Cider and *caramel apple cupcakes*: The crisp sweetness of sparkling apple cider complements the rich, buttery flavor of caramel apple cupcakes for a refreshing fall-inspired treat.

Chai Tea and *pumpkin spice cupcakes*: The warm, spiced flavors of chai tea enhance the cinnamon and nutmeg notes in pumpkin spice cupcakes, creating a cozy, comforting pairing.

Iced Coffee and *chocolate mocha cupcakes*: For coffee lovers, pairing iced coffee with a chocolate mocha cupcake intensifies the chocolatey richness while adding a refreshing coffee twist.

Vanilla Bean Milkshake and *cookies and cream cupcakes*: This creamy and indulgent combination brings out the nostalgic flavors of cookies and cream while adding a velvety smooth finish.

Hot Chocolate and *peppermint cupcakes*: The rich, cocoa flavor of hot chocolate pairs perfectly with a peppermint cupcake, making this duo a delightful wintertime treat.

Strawberry Lemonade and *lemon cupcakes*: The bright, zesty flavor of lemon cupcakes pairs beautifully with the sweet-tart balance of strawberry lemonade, creating a refreshing, summery combination.

Herbal Chamomile Tea and *honey cupcakes*: The light floral notes of chamomile tea perfectly complement the delicate sweetness of honey cupcakes for a calming, soothing pairing.

So, whether you're hosting a gathering with friends, celebrating a personal milestone, or simply treating yourself to something sweet, I hope these pairings inspire you to find your own perfect match—both in the kitchen and in life. Thank you so much for reading **Cupcakes & Romance**, and I can't wait to share more stories of love, faith, and sweet moments with you in the future!

Until then, happy baking, sipping, and romancing!

With gratitude,

Abiegail Rose

BY ABIEGAIL ROSE
WHEN BEAUTY
BREAKS
A PSYCHOSPIRITUAL PARANORMAL THRILLER

When Beauty Breaks

A Psychospiritual Paranormal Thriller

"When beauty becomes a curse, fame is the price I can no longer afford."

Beauty is fleeting. This was a truth woven into the fabric of my upbringing, like the delicate threads of a cherished family tapestry. I remember my mother's gentle voice, barely audible over the hum of the Sunday morning congregation, as she whispered those words like a persistent prayer.

"Remember, sweetheart, beauty is fleeting."

My mother believed it with all her heart. She lived by it. But I...
I didn't listen.

I was too focused on the reflection in the mirror, captivated by the shimmering image of perfection that stared back at me. I craved the compliments, the instant gratification of a hundred likes on social media, and those ephemeral moments when people saw me and thought I was someone worth admiring.

Somewhere along that path, I traded in my mother's whispers for the thunderous applause of the world. Faith surrendered to fame; my soul was sacrificed for beauty.

This is a story about how that choice destroyed me.

But it's not just about vanity. It's about control—about wanting to be more than what I am, to be seen, adored, praised. It's about the insatiable yearning that gnaws away at one's very being until everything else—morals, relationships, identity—is stripped away like dead leaves in a storm.

It's about making a deal with dark forces for eternal youth and beauty only to see that desire twist and decay until all that remains is an empty reflection.

Because beauty is fragile. For all its power, it doesn't last. And once you've sold your soul for it, there's no going back—or so

I thought.

Before you read this story, remember: Not everything that glitters is gold. Sometimes, it hides something far darker beneath its seductive surface.

Pre-Order Today on Barnes & Noble, Amazon and other Major Retailers by visiting Books2Read.com/WhenBeautyBreaks

What People Are Saying...

"When Beauty Breaks is a haunting and emotionally charged novel that echoes the timeless themes of Oscar Wilde's The Picture of Dorian Gray while plunging deep into the modern world of social media, celebrity, and the fragile pursuit of perfection."

"A modern-day gothic masterpiece."

"Abiegail brilliantly captures the dark side of modern beauty culture, crafting a story that feels like a cautionary tale for our times."

"A gripping meditation on the dangers of vanity and the fleet-

ing nature of social media-driven fame."

Pre-Order Today on Barnes & Noble, Amazon and other

Major Retailers by visiting Books2Read.com/WhenBeauty-

Breaks

EDGE OF OBLIVION

ABIEGAIL ROSE

Edge of Oblivion

The Revelation Chronicles
Book 1

In a world teetering on the edge of destruction, the fabric of society unravels as a new global power takes control. As darkness spreads and hope seems all but lost, a few brave souls must confront the harsh reality of the times, where every choice carries eternal consequences.

Amidst the chaos, Caleb and Rachel find themselves facing unimaginable trials. Caleb, torn between doubt and faith, is thrust into a conflict that challenges everything he once believed. Rachel, driven by her unwavering conviction, holds fast to the promise of something greater beyond the suffering.

As the forces of good and evil clash, those who remain must decide which side they stand on. The stakes are higher than survival—this is a fight for the soul of humanity, and time is running out.

The Revelation Chronicles is an epic journey of courage, faith, and the relentless battle for truth in a world consumed by deception. The end is near, but what lies beyond is yet to be revealed.

Read today on Barnes & Noble, Amazon and other Major Retailers by visiting Books2Read.com/edgeofoblivion

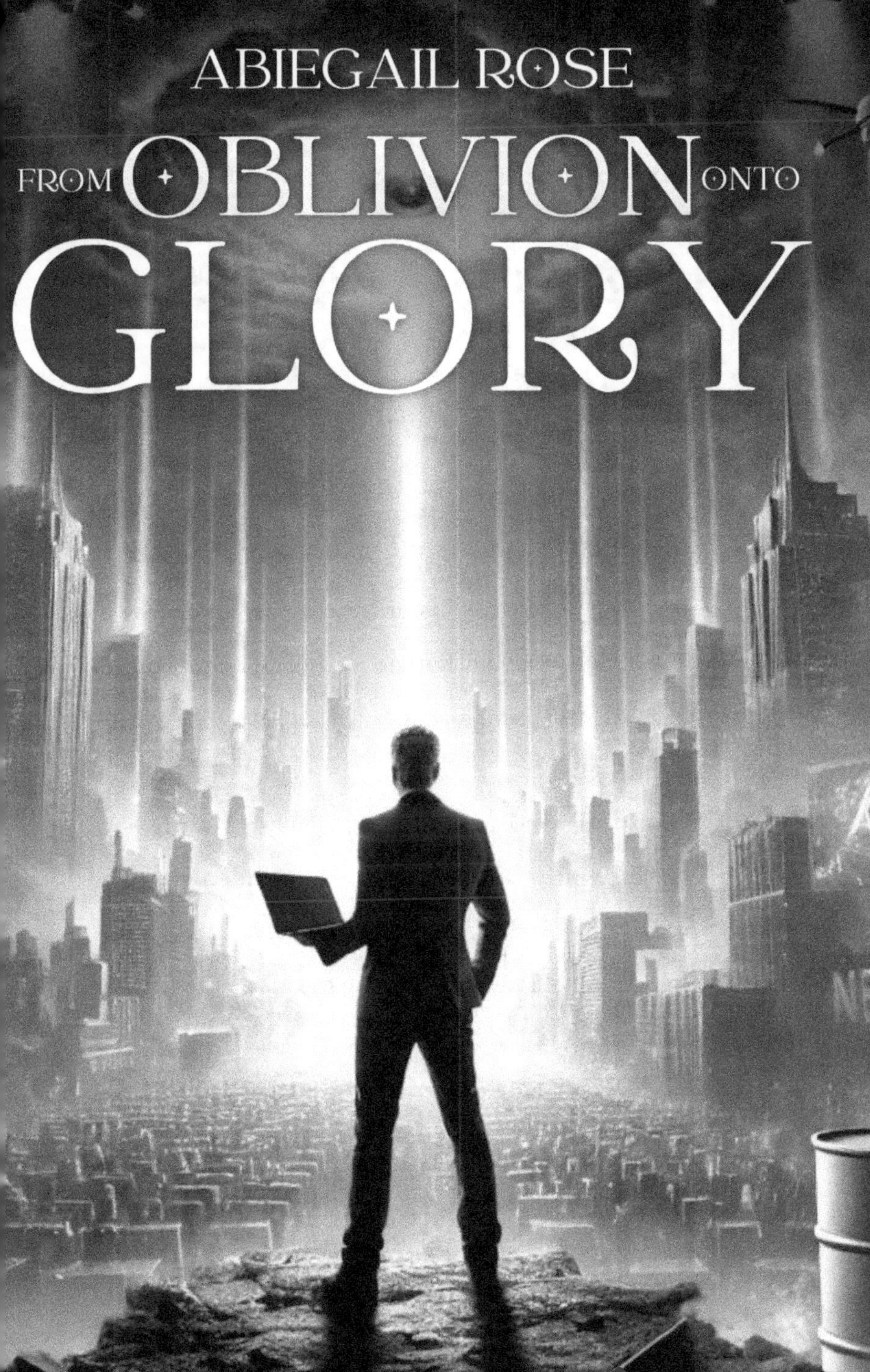

ABIEGAIL ROSE
FROM OBLIVION ONTO
GLORY

From Oblivion onto Glory

The Revelation Chronicles
Book 2

Caleb thought he had escaped his nightmare, but when millions of Christians mysteriously die and a new world order rises, he realizes his darkest fears are only just beginning. Now, caught in the Tribulation, he finds himself battling forces far beyond anything he imagined—and his greatest enemy may be himself.

As the world falls under the iron grip of a new leader, Caleb discovers a purpose that pushes him to the edge of faith and beyond. Using his skills as a programmer, he infiltrates the global social media systems, sharing the gospel with those still searching for hope. But in a world where every move is monitored and every message controlled, his mission becomes increasingly dangerous.

Caleb faces a choice: continue hiding in the shadows or risk everything to stand for the truth—even if it means paying the ultimate price. Yet, even death may not be the end, because beyond the chaos, beyond the suffering, lies the promise of something greater: where all things are made new.

Can Caleb rise from the ashes of oblivion and become a beacon of light in the darkest of times? Or will he fall into the hands of those who seek to destroy the truth?

Pre-order *From Oblivion onto Glory* today by visiting Book s2Read.com/OblivionOntoGlory and follow Caleb's harrowing journey through the Tribulation. Secure your copy now and be among the first to experience the gripping sequel to *Edge of Oblivion*—a story of faith, courage, and the eternal battle between light and darkness.

Don't wait—eternity is at stake.

Visit www.books2read.com/oblivionontoglory to reserve your copy today!

Also by Abiegail Rose

<u>Thrillers & Suspense</u>

When Beauty Breaks: A Psychospiritual Paranormal
Thriller

Edge of Oblivion

Oblivion onto Glory

Armored in Faith – Coming December

<u>Sweet & Clean Romance</u>

Ace's Heart: An Ex-Mafia, 2ndChance, Christian Romance

Cupcakes & Romance

Love & Decay: A Zombpocalypse Romance (Kindle Vella)

<u>Motivational</u>

Let Your Light Shine : Rocking Your Purpose, Living Your Passion

Blessed Nourishment Vol. 1

49 Days of Self-Discovery

Prince, Not Required: Slaying your inner dragons, without dropping your crown!

Business

Love Lessons in Marketing: How Love Story Tropes Can Elevate Your Brand

Boss Babe Publishing: The Ultimate Self-Publishing Guide and Workbook

The Carter Effect: Hip-Hop 101

Boss Babe by Design

Children's Books

Duke's Puppy Manners Series

The Lost Chronicles of Light Series

Abiegail Rose

Abiegail Rose is an author known for weaving tales of passion, heartache, and ultimate triumph. With a gift for creating unforgettable characters and immersive stories, Abiegail's novels have captured the hearts of readers around the globe, earning her a loyal following.

Born with a love for storytelling, Abiegail began her writing journey at a young age, filling notebooks with tales of romance and adventure. Her unique ability to tap into the emotional depths of her characters has made her a standout voice in the romance genre, with each book exploring the complexities of love in its many forms.

In addition to her success as an author, Abiegail has a background in marketing, where she discovered the powerful parallels between crafting compelling love stories and creating engaging brand narratives. This realization inspired her to write *Love Lessons in Marketing: How Love Story Tropes Can Elevate Your Brand Strategy*, blending her two passions into a guide that helps brands connect with their audiences on a deeply emotional level.

When she's not writing, Abiegail enjoys traveling, indulging in classic romance novels, and exploring the latest trends in marketing and storytelling. She lives with her family in the Houston-Metro, where she continues to dream up new stories that inspire, entertain, and remind us all of the power of love.

Want to join her book club to be first in line for new releases? Visit https://authorabiegailrose.com/

Follow her on Instagram @authorabiegailrose

Follow her on Goodreads
https://www.goodreads.com/abiegailrose

Follow her on Amazon
http://amazon.com/author/abiegailrose

Get a signed book: http://authorabiegailrose.com